W9-BTA-520

The Princess
and the Pea

adapted & illustrated by

Alain Vaës

Little, Brown and Company

BOSTON   NEW YORK   LONDON

First Edition

Library of Congress Cataloging-in-Publication Data

Vaës, Alain.
     The princess and the pea / adapted and illustrated by Alain
Vaës. — 1st ed.
        p. cm.
     Summary: In this adaptation of "The Princess and the Pea," the
prince is ready for marriage, but the queen is more concerned
with her jewelry collection.
     ISBN 0-316-89633-0
     [1. Fairy tales. 2. Jewelry — Fiction. 3. Humorous stories.] I.
Andersen, H. C. (Hans Christian), 1805–1875. Prindsessen paa
ærten. English. II. Title.

PZ8.V13 Pr 2001
[E]   00-048378

10 9 8 7 6 5 4 3 2 1

TWP

Printed in Singapore

To Annabelle

The land of Crestalia was divided into two kingdoms.

There was Lower Crestalia, which no one knew or cared much about. And there was Upper Crestalia, home to King Adolph, Queen Frieda, and their only child, Prince Ralph.

The king cared little for ruling the land. He left that up to the queen. Her main interest was her jewelry collection. She loved every kind of precious gem — except one.

"Opals! Yuck! I can't bear them," she said. "A gypsy once told me that an opal would change my life. I like my life the way it is, thank you."

So the queen went on thinking about gems. The more the queen thought about them, the more she wanted to own them all. Then one day while she was admiring a ruby, Prince Ralph entered his mother's bedchamber.

"Mother, there's something on my mind," he said.

"What is it?" she asked. She was very fond of her son . . . as long as he didn't disturb her gem collection.

He blurted it all out. He'd been talking with his father, and . . . and . . . well, he knew a lot more about grown-up men and women than when he was younger. The result was, he said, "I want to get married."

The queen paled. She thought about how much money a royal wedding would cost. And before that, the prince might even want to have one of *her* gems, perhaps a diamond, for an engagement ring. "This is quite sudden," she said slowly. "There's so much to consider." Then, in a flash, she had an idea. If there were no more weddings or engagements, hardly anyone would want those stray diamonds and gems that lay in jewelry stores. Except her, of course. She could buy them all up for a few pennies, and her collection would grow and grow.

"Let me see what I can do," said the queen, and she smiled coldly.

At dinner, she revealed her plan. "We're going to issue a proclamation to nearby kingdoms announcing a search for a wife for our son and heir. I'll personally look over the applications. Oh, and by the way, until the prince takes a wife, we simply won't allow anyone else to do so, either. No engagements or weddings until Prince Ralph's future is assured."

King Adolph nodded assent. He was more interested in his pudding than in what she said. But the prince was overjoyed at the news.

The proclamation was posted throughout the land. Within days, the palace was flooded with applicants. The queen sorted through them and picked the top three.

On the morning of the interviews, the full court gathered to watch.

The first contestant — a beautiful, tall redhead — entered the room.

"Hmm, Princess Tiffany," said the queen, scanning the application. "You attended good schools and are studying biologic anthropology. Well, today's test is in two parts. First, please put on this blindfold. Then show us that you can do backward then forward hopscotch without touching a line. Begin!"

The princess threw the little stone at "Home." She took a deep breath and hopped, skipped, and jumped her way back and forth as ordered. Not one line was smudged.

"Very well," said the queen, reaching into a glass bowl and pulling out a slip of paper. "Now you have ten seconds to answer this question: If you break a mirror, how many years of bad luck will it bring?"

The princess hesitated. Then, on the tenth second, she cried, "One?"

"Wrong! . . . Seven!" said the queen. "Next!"

Prince Ralph sighed as Tiffany left. But he smiled when a petite blonde princess came through the door.

"Princess Penelope," began the queen. "You're an expert in the field of solar ethnicology. Let's see how well you do at the following. Here are two yo-yos. Please demonstrate, in order, walking two dogs, going around the world, and rocking the baby."

The princess took the yo-yos. She wrapped their strings around her fingers. Then she went through the paces — with no mistakes.

"All right, I suppose," said the queen, pulling out a slip from the glass bowl. "Now all you have to do is fill in the last line of this safety rule: 'Cross on the green, not . . .' What is the rest of it?"

"Oh, I know, I know," said the princess eagerly. "Not on the red."

"Wrong! The answer is 'Not in between.' Next!" snapped the queen.

Prince Ralph groaned. So did the rest of the court. Then a tall princess with jet-black hair entered and bowed to the queen. She was the last hope.

"Ah, yes, Princess Francine," said the queen, holding the bowl firmly. "You're in charge of a secret cyberspace-ecology project. So, here are two rubber bands. Show us the complete cycle of cat's cradle, spider's web, and rock the hammock."

The princess flexed her fingers and began. She stretched, she groaned, she twisted — and she did it.

"All right," said the queen. "Now, just answer this question in ten seconds. Why did the chicken cross the road?"

The princess gazed into space, frowned, then replied, "To find something to eat?"

"Sorry, wrong! To get to the other side," said the queen. "Good-bye! Thank you. Court adjourned."

Prince Ralph shouted, "Now I'll never have a wife!" and stormed out along with the rest of the court.

The prince got into his car and drove off into the countryside. As he reached the Lower Crestalia border, he started to smell smoke. The car slowed and then stopped. When the prince raised the hood, a dark cloud told him something was very wrong, something he couldn't fix.

The prince sat by the side of the road feeling very sorry for himself: no wife, no car, no happiness.

But fortunately, a few minutes later a dented, rusty pickup truck came by and stopped. A young woman in overalls jumped out. She had OVH embroidered on her pocket.

She checked under the hood and said, "Fan belt. Hand me that wrench."

With his help, she had it all fixed in a few minutes. When she took off her kerchief to wipe her face, the prince saw a long braid coiled around her head, like a crown.

Pointing to the initials on her overalls, he asked, "Is that your company's name?"

"Nope. Mine. Opaline von Highbredde," she said. "But you can call me Opal, 'cause of this." She showed him a large opal worn on a gold chain around her neck. "Actually," she said casually, "I'm the crown princess of Lower Crestalia. I'm just doing this trucking thing until I come of age."

Prince Ralph looked at her again. Suddenly he saw through the grease and grime. She really was beautiful. And she was a genuine princess!

The princess, catching his eye, realized she liked having someone gaze at her like that.

"You have to come with me right now," he said. He swept her into his car and told her all about the proclamation, the tests, and how he wanted her to be his bride.

"This is kind of sudden," she said. But looking at the prince, she knew that this was the man of her dreams. She became determined to pass the tests.

At first Queen Frieda refused to interview this late applicant. But the king, waking from a nap, yawned and said he thought his son's idea was splendid. Since her husband made so few demands, the queen couldn't refuse him.

Without even asking the princess's name, the queen got down to business.

"You understand the rules? You must pass two tests. One failure or wrong answer and you're out on your ear!" she said.

The princess rubbed her hands against her overalls and said, "Ready."

The queen snapped her fingers, summoning two maids with long ropes.

"All right," she said. "Let's see you do one hundred double Dutch jumps using only one leg. Begin!"

The jump ropes snapped, the contest began. The princess threw out her arms for balance and went to it. *Bam! Bam! Bam!*

In less than two minutes, the princess completed the full one hundred jumps.

Angrily, the queen fished into the glass bowl and pulled out another slip of paper.

"All right," she said. "Ten seconds for an answer to this. What's worse than biting into an apple and finding a worm in it? Ten . . . nine . . . eight . . . seven . . ."

"Finding half a worm!" shouted the princess, slapping her thigh.

There was absolute silence. Then the court burst into applause. Prince Ralph rushed toward the princess to take her hand.

"Not so fast," said the queen. "I've decided that there's one more test. We'll discuss it tomorrow morning. Now I must go and prepare the guest room."

"What's this other test?" asked the king, following her into the guest room. He watched as the queen had twenty soft and fluffy goose-down mattresses placed on the bed.

"We can't have our son marry just anyone," said the queen, slipping a tiny green pea between the bottom two mattresses. "A royal princess must be truly sensitive. This pea should prevent any real princess from getting a decent night's sleep. If she sleeps well, then she's a fraud!"

After a long dinner served with lots of warm milk, the princess went off to the guest bedroom. Yawning, she uncoiled her long braid, swung her head, and let her hair hang down without the usual brushing. She didn't notice that her opal had caught itself in her hair and was dangling down her back.

With a huge yawn, she settled into bed . . . but something began to bother her. There was a lump in the middle of her back. She twisted and turned, but it was always there. There was no way she could sleep, so she pulled a notebook from her tool bag and started scribbling notes about things she thought the queen might ask. Arithmetic. Spelling. History. Geography. Science. Car repair. The names of all the kings and queens of Upper and Lower Crestalia. The Great War.

She was still writing when breakfast was announced. Splashing some water on her face, she tucked away her notebook and went off to face the final test.

The royal family was already seated at the breakfast table when she got there.

"Did you get a good night's sleep?" the queen asked sweetly.

"I don't want to complain, but I was up all night. There was something underneath me," said the princess. "Hey, wait a minute. Now I see it might have been my —"

But before she could finish, the prince said, "There, she's passed the final test. Mother, please welcome my bride, the crown princess of Lower Crestalia, Princess Opaline von Highbredde."

"Opal. . . . Oh, no, Opal!" shrieked the queen.

"There it is," said the princess, untangling her braid. "My necklace. You see, the opal is a lucky jewel in my country. But to tell the truth, our royal treasury is loaded with others — diamonds, rubies, sapphires. I inherit them all next month, when I come of age."

"All those precious gems! Yours?" gasped the queen. She thought a moment. "No . . . ours!"

"Welcome daughter!"

She embraced the princess and announced, "We must make plans for a royal wedding. My darling girl, come with me. We must talk about an engagement ring. Do you have anything suitable?"

The king smiled. The prince beamed. And the two royal ladies walked off arm in arm. It was a clear sign that in Upper Crestalia and Lower Crestalia, all would live happily ever after.